Katie Woo

No More Teasing

by Fran Manushkin

illustrated by Tammie Lyon

raintree

a Capstone company — publishers for children

Raintree is an imprint of Capstone Global Library Limited, a company
incorporated in England and Wales having its registered office at 264 Banbury
Road, Oxford, OX2 7DY – Registered company number: 6695582

www.raintree.co.uk
myorders@raintree.co.uk

Text © Capstone Global Library Limited 2019
The moral rights of the proprietor have been asserted.

Creative Director: Heather Kindseth
Graphic Designer: Emily Harris
Printed and bound in India

ISBN 978 1 4747 8219 7
23 22 21 20 19
10 9 8 7 6 5 4 3 2 1

British Library Cataloguing in Publication Data
A full catalogue record for this book is available from
the British Library.

Acknowledgements
Fran Manushkin, pg. 26
Tammie Lyon, pg. 26

Contents

Chapter 1
Mean Roddy

One day, on the way to school, Katie Woo tripped. She fell into the mud. Splat!

She scraped her knee, and

mud got on her new jumper

and all of her books.

Katie started

to cry.

"Cry baby! Cry baby!"

yelled Roddy Rogers.

Katie's feelings were so

hurt, she cried even more.

Roddy grinned.

At school, Roddy Rogers

kept teasing Katie during

break.

"Go away!" she told him.

But Roddy didn't.

At lunch,

they had pizza,

Katie's favourite.

   She took such a big bite

that she got tomato sauce on

her nose and cheeks.

"Look at Katie," Roddy shouted. "Katie's got a filthy face!"

Roddy said, "Filthy face! Filthy face!"

"Stop it!" cried Katie. But Roddy didn't stop. He was having too much fun.

Roddy made

faces at Katie all

day long.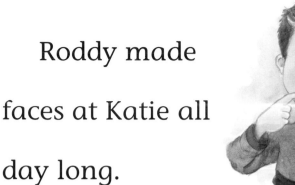

When Katie stuck

her tongue out at him, he

made more faces. Ugly ones.

"How can I make Roddy

stop teasing me?" Katie

asked her friend JoJo.

But JoJo didn't know.

Chapter 2

The amazing butterfly

The next day, Roddy

teased Katie when she was

running at break. And he

teased her when she was

trying to read her book.

Katie was so unhappy. She
didn't want to go to school
any more.

The next day, Miss Winkle told the class, "Everyone, our butterflies are ready to hatch. Please hurry over and watch them!"

Katie pushed up her glasses.

"Hey, I see four eyes!"

Roddy said in a quiet voice.

He knew if Miss Winkle heard

him, he would get in trouble.

Katie was about to

say something back. But

suddenly, her butterfly began

hatching.

It was so amazing. She

couldn't take her eyes off it!

Roddy said, "Four eyes!" a
bit louder.

But Katie kept watching
her butterfly.

Roddy was so cross. He
slammed his desk and hurt
his finger.

Chapter 3
Stop teasing!

Later, the class worked

on their "Good Neighbours"

paintings with a partner.

Roddy sneaked over to

Katie and said, "Eurgh! Your

painting is ugly!"

But Katie loved painting so

much that she kept doing it.

"Hey!" Roddy said. "Didn't

you hear me?"

Katie still didn't answer.

Roddy got so cross that he
smeared black paint all over
his part of his picture.

"Hey!" his partner yelled.
"You've ruined our painting!"

On the way home, Roddy

glared at Katie, but she

didn't even look at him.

Katie began smiling

and smiling.

When JoJo sat down,

Katie told her, "I'm so happy!

I know how to make Roddy

stop teasing me."

"What do you do?"

asked JoJo.

About the author

Fran Manushkin is the author of many popular picture books, including *Baby, Come Out!*; *Latkes and Applesauce: A Hanukkah Story*; *The Belly Book* and *Big Girl Panties*. There is a real Katie Woo - she's Fran's great-niece - but she never gets in half the trouble that Katie Woo does in the books. Fran writes on her beloved Mac computer in New York City, USA, without the help of her two naughty cats, Chaim and Goldy.

About the illustrator

Tammie Lyon began her love for drawing at a young age while sitting at the kitchen table with her dad. She continued her love of art and eventually attended college, where she earned a bachelors degree in fine art. After a brief career as a professional ballet dancer, she decided to devote herself full time to illustration. Today she lives with her husband, Lee, in Cincinnati, Ohio, USA. Her dogs, Gus and Dudley, keep her company as she works in her studio.

 Glossary

amazing causing sudden surprise or wonder

favourite the thing that is liked best

filthy dirty

hatching breaking out of an egg or cocoon

ruined spoiled or destroyed something

smeared rubbed something over a surface, making it messy

 Discussion questions

1. Katie was so sad when she fell in the mud. What could you have said to make her feel better?

2. What do you think Miss Winkle would have done if she heard Roddy calling Katie names?

3. Katie worked out a great way to get Roddy to stop teasing her. Are there other ways she could have made him stop?

 # Writing prompts

1. Roddy was not being a good classmate. Write down three rules that could help him be a better classmate.

2. The children were painting "Good Neighbours" pictures. What sort of things could go in this type of painting? Write a list.

3. Roddy is a bully. Write down five words that describe a bully.

Having fun with Katie Woo

In *No More Teasing,* Katie Woo's class is working on "Good Neighbours" paintings. It is fun to make a piece of art with other people. Try making a poster with a partner and practise working together.

What you need:

- a large piece of cardboard. It should be big enough that both of you can gather around it.
- art supplies like pencils, felt tips, crayons, paints, etc.

Getting started

1. Decide what your picture's theme will be. You should both agree on a theme together.

2. Divide the poster into sections. Each of you will get your own area to work on. You might also want to save a section for words that describe your theme. For example, "Our favourite animals" describes a pet theme.

3. Before you start drawing, talk to your partner about what you will each draw. You might also want to talk about which colours you will use. That way your sections will look nice together.

4. Now start drawing and painting! Before you know it, your teamwork will result in a beautiful poster.